I Got This!

My Dragon Books - Volume 8

Steve Herman

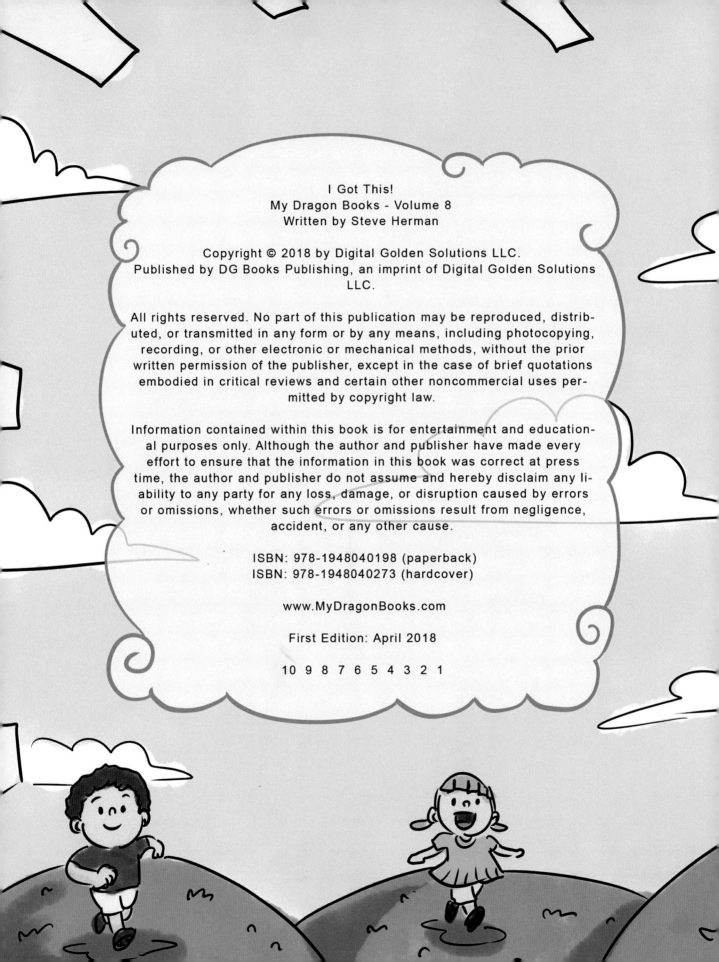

I Got This!
My Dragon Books - Volume 8
Written by Steve Herman

ISBN: 978-1948040198 (paperback)
ISBN: 978-1948040273 (hardcover)

www.MyDragonBooks.com

First Edition: April 2018

10 9 8 7 6 5 4 3 2 1

Diggory learns his lessons fast –
He really is quite smart,
And when it's tough, he tries his best;
bless his little heart!

First, I taught him lots of tricks
and how to use the potty...

"The fight will end with your best friend
when you apologize."

Diggory loves the playground;
it's his favorite place to be,

But when we must go home, he gets real mad at me.

There's a big, mean bully, and he goes to Diggory's school.

"If you want to beat a bully, just be nice when he is rude; It's nothing you can't handle with a proper attitude."

Diggory Doo is lazy,
and he avoids doing chores –
He'd rather skip the work
so he can play outdoors.

When Diggory has a lot of work,
it's hard to get it done;
He says he has too much to do,
and that's not any fun.

"Diggory, you can do this! Just take it slow and steady."

When he can't find his favorite toy, Diggory gets annoyed...

"You can handle your frustration –
You're a great big boy!"

I tell him when unhappy thoughts creep inside his head...

"I know that you can overcome –
think happy thoughts, instead."

Diggory gets impatient
when he must wait in line;
He pouts and stamps his foot,
and then he starts to whine.

Diggory goes to dragon school
to learn things he should know,
But when his lessons get too tough,
he doesn't want to go.

Get your FREE Gift from Diggory Doo at
www.MyDragonBooks.com/gift

Read more about Drew and Diggory Doo!

Visit
www.MyDragonBooks.com
for more!

Manufactured by Amazon.ca
Bolton, ON

13334208R00033